JIM ELDRIDGE

SURVIVOR

ESCAPE FROM POMPEII

■ SCHOLASTIC

PROLOGUE

24 AUGUST AD 79
POMPEII

I hurried to the square in Pompeii and saw eight priests, standing in a circle, offering loud prayers to the god Vulcan. Next to them was a pile of wooden crates, each with squawking chickens inside. Standing by the crates was a soldier with a knife in his hand. A crowd had gathered round the priests.

Then I saw my father. He was climbing up on a plinth. A statue had fallen off the plinth and lay broken beside it.

To my horror, he began to shout at the priests and the people.

"People of Pompeii, listen to me! This earthquake is nothing to do with Vulcan. Vulcan does not exist!" As the people turned away from the priests and looked towards my father, horrified by his words, he pointed towards the mountain, Vesuvius.

"This earthquake is caused by the fires raging under Vesuvius. There is nothing you, or the priests, can do about it. Vesuvius will explode. And when it does it will shower this city with hot ash. Rivers of fire will pour down from the mountain. You will all die unless you leave now and get to higher ground away from the mountain. Flee!"

There were loud shouts of anger from the crowd, as they began throwing rocks at my father and shouting: "Silence him! It is his fault! He insulted Vulcan!"

The rocks hit my father and he fell backwards onto the cobbles. I ran to help him up, as others also rushed towards him, some arming themselves with wooden sticks.

My father scrambled to his feet, grabbed me by the hand and dragged me into a side street. He was bleeding from a gash in his head where a stone had hit him.

"We have to make people see the truth, Marcus!" he panted. "We have to save them!"

"No!" I shouted at him. And now I felt tears stinging my eyes. "They're right! This earthquake is all your fault. You have insulted Vulcan! I hate you! I hate you!"

And with that, I ran away from him as fast as I could.

Hot flakes rained down. The earth shook. Buildings cracked and fell. People cried out in fear and ran.

CHAPTER

Our small two-wheeled cart trundled along the winding country road, pulled by our old horse, Pallas. We were on our way to Pompeii. It's a journey that my father, Lucius, and I do every year. We travel from our small cottage in the country, twenty miles outside Pompeii, to celebrate the Festival of Augustus with my father's brother and his family: my Uncle Castus, Aunt Drusilla and their six-year-old twins, Fabius and Julia.

There are lots of festivals throughout the year,

mostly in praise of the gods to keep them happy with us. The gods are all-powerful and there are hundreds of them, each one ruling a different part of life. There is Neptune, who controls the sea; Mars, the god of war; Venus, the goddess of love; Vulcan, the god of fire and volcanoes. Vulcan lives in a huge cave, deep beneath the earth, where he hammers at his forge making gates to control the fires that rage underground. Over them all is Jupiter, king of all the gods. We don't attend many of the festivals to celebrate the gods. My father says he doesn't believe in the gods. He says things happen because of nature, not because gods cause them to happen. I wish he wouldn't talk this way, but he does. Sometimes I think he says things like this just to annoy people. Other times I think he does it because he is mad. The priests have warned him not to say such terrible things – they believe that the gods will take revenge on him.

Uncle Castus says that my father became crazy when my mother was killed in an earthquake ten years ago. I was just two years old at the time. I can't remember much about my mother. I remember the warm smell of her when she cuddled me, but that is about all.

After the earthquake my father was left to bring me up on his own.

My mother's death made him so angry he began to speak out against the gods, saying they must hate humans to kill us like that. Then he started saying that there were no such things as gods. He said everything that happened was a natural thing: earthquakes, rain, volcanoes and storms – they were nothing to do with the gods. He said if we learned to understand nature we could stop these dreadful things happening.

At first people laughed at him, but when he carried on saying things like that the priests said he was mad and dangerous and would be locked up if he didn't shut up.

But my father didn't shut up. And they didn't lock him up. So he carried on saying the same mad things.

The trouble was other children didn't want to be friends with me, because of my father.

When he wasn't saying mad things about the gods, my father worked as a land engineer. It started because of his obsession with earthquakes and volcanoes – trying to find out how and why they happened. He studied how different plants grew better in different soils, how water drained faster from some places than it did from others, and everything else to do with land. The result was that farmers and landowners hired him to get the best crops from their fields.

And they were glad to pay him, until inevitably the subject of the gods would come up. They would ask him which gods they should sacrifice to in order to get the best harvest, or to make their lambs and goats grow faster. When they did this, my father would start his rant about how there were no such things as the gods. When he did that, the farmers would tell him they no longer wanted him on their land – they believed if he stayed, the gods would punish them.

That was why we never had much money. Every time he started a new job, it would go wrong. By the time I was eight my father had the reputation of a madman, and no one would hire him. So we lived in our small house. My father fed us with fruit and vegetables he grew, and we both cut wood to keep the fires warm.

Now and then we'd travel to Pompeii to visit my uncle and his family, and stay the night with them before travelling back home. Or sometimes we'd go to Herculaneum, the next big town. I was always glad when we did this because it was fun to be in a busy town, with the markets and lots of people bustling around.

At this time of year we travelled to Pompeii twice: once for the festival of the harvest, celebrating the crops being gathered in, and again for today's festival celebrating Augustus, the first and greatest emperor of Rome. It was Augustus who created the Roman Empire, which rules the whole world.

Yesterday had been the Vulcanalia, when sacrifices and prayers were said for the god Vulcan. This is why I thought it was strange when I felt the ground begin to shake beneath me. There had been other signs on our journey that showed that Vulcan was unhappy: the sound of thunder from beneath the earth; smoke coming from the mountain, Vesuvius. Vesuvius was just two miles from where we were, and towered over the landscape. We often had small earthquakes and earth tremors, but these seemed stronger than usual.

Why was Vulcan so angry? Had yesterday's festival not been to his liking?

Pallas, our old horse, stopped suddenly while pulling our cart along the country road. He stood, trembling, his ears laid back in fear.

"Vulcan is angry," I said.

"There is no Vulcan, Marcus," said my father. "Haven't you listened to anything I've told you? This earthquake being is caused by the volcano, Vesuvius, not by a god."

"Shut up!" I shouted angrily at him. "The gods will strike you down for saying that!"

Suddenly there was a huge tremor and a crack appeared in the road ahead of us. Pallas let out a frightened neigh and reared back.

There was the sound of an explosion from Vesuvius. Huge rocks began to roll down the mountain, some of them heading straight for us. A massive boulder bounced from a field and hit our cart. My father and I were hurled out onto the road. I was just scrambling to my feet when I saw another huge boulder hurtling towards us.

CRASH!

My father and I just managed to dodge to one side, but the boulder smashed into the cart. I saw Pallas fall to the ground. As I ran towards him, I could see that our old horse was dead.

CHAPTER

I was standing looking down at poor Pallas and thinking that this was Vulcan's revenge for what my father had said, when I heard my father call out, "Marcus, look at this!"

I turned and saw that he had run into a field. I ran after him, and saw that there were sheep lying on the ground.

"They're dead!" he shouted. This seemed to make him happy, which I thought was odd. But then, a lot of what my father did was odd.

"Smell that air, Marcus!"

I did. It stank. It was like the smell of bad eggs, but much worse. And it was hot.

"That's what killed these sheep. The smell is coming from holes where the ground has cracked open. It's coming from the fires under the ground. The fire from the volcano is spreading beneath the earth. It proves I'm right! We must hurry to Pompeii and warn the people!"

"Warn them about what?"

"That the volcano is building up to an eruption. If that happens, Pompeii will be in danger. Come on, Marcus! We have to hurry!"

"We can't go anywhere," I said. "The cart is broken and Pallas is dead!"

I looked again at our poor dead horse. I felt tears come to my eyes as I remembered all the happy times I'd spent with him: walking behind him as we ploughed our small field, and riding him as he trotted gently along.

"We can run! shouted my father. "We aren't far from Pompeii."

He started to run along the road towards the city.

I shook my head in disbelief. I couldn't understand how he could be so heartless about Pallas! But when my father got obsessed, he didn't pay attention to anything else; not to me, not to Pallas, not even to our home. I ran after him.

"No, father! Please stop saying these things!" I pleaded.

"But I'm right!" he said as we ran. "The bad smell shows that gases are being forced out from under the ground. It's caused by pressure from the volcano. With that sort of pressure building up, Vesuvius is going to explode. And when it does, all that fire will come out in rivers of hot rock. They will pour down on Pompeii. We have to warn the people that they must leave the city."

"No! Father, stop! Please just stop." I shouted. "This is happening because Vulcan is angry. The mountain is shaking because something must have gone wrong at the Vulcanalia yesterday. That's what the priests say, and they know about this sort of thing! Earthquakes happen all the time, but they don't mean that a volcano is going to blow up."

My father shook his head.

"This one is different. The priests are wrong. Prayers and sacrifices won't stop the mountain blowing up and killing everyone. Even if the people won't listen to me, we must get my brother and his family to safety."

He carried on running. As always, I felt angry at the way he embarrassed us by insisting he was right and everyone else was wrong. Why couldn't he just be normal? I was sure the priests would find a way to make Vulcan happy and Vesuvius would settle down.

But then I thought of the earthquake that had killed my mother, and so many others, ten years ago. If things did get worse, then we had to help my uncle and aunt and my two little cousins to safety.

I ran after my father, towards Pompeii.

CHAPTER

3

Things were getting worse as we reached Pompeii. The ground was shaking more and more. It seemed worse in the city than it had in the country because the buildings looked as if they were about to fall down at any moment. Some big statues had already toppled over and I saw two drinking fountains that had cracked open. Water was pouring out of them and running down the street.

There were also strange flakes falling from the sky, like big snowflakes. Only these flakes were grey and warm.

"What are these?" I asked my father, picking up a handful of the flakes from the ground.

"They're from inside the mountain," he said.

I looked at Vesuvius and saw that a big cloud of smoke was rising up from it and spreading out. These flakes must have come up in the cloud and then carried to Pompeii on the wind.

Now, for the first time, I began to feel worried. I'd felt earthquakes and tremors before, but I'd never known flakes like this to come from the mountain.

It looked like people were starting to panic. Some were rushing out of their houses because they were worried they might collapse on them, others were kneeling down in the street offering loud prayers to Vulcan, begging him to stop the earth shaking.

When we reached my uncle's house, Uncle Castus and Aunt Drusilla were inside. They were packing a few belongings, helped by my cousins Fabius and Julia.

"Castus!" shouted my father.

"Greetings, Lucius," said my uncle. "Welcome. And you too, Marcus. I hope you are well."

"You have to leave the city!" my father urged them.

"Vesuvius is about to explode. This whole city will be destroyed!"

"Calm yourself," said my uncle. "It's nothing more than a few tremors. You know it's always been like this. The priests are taking care of it."

"They are in the square right now offering a sacrifice of twelve chickens to Vulcan," said Aunt Drusilla.

"Then why are you packing?" demanded my father.

"In case it takes a little longer," said Uncle Castus, smiling calmly at the children. "We will stay in a wooden shed until the tremors are over."

"No, you must leave the city!" shouted my father. "Otherwise you will all die!"

At this, my little cousins looked absolutely terrified and began to cry. As Aunt Drusilla went to comfort them, my uncle grabbed my father by the arm and dragged him roughly into another room. I followed.

"Stop it!" Castus snapped at my father. "Pull yourself together. You are scaring Fabius and Julia. You heard what I said, the priests are dealing with it."

"They can't deal with this, Castus. The mountain is going to explode! I have seen the signs." And he started to tell him about the dead sheep and the smell in the fields.

"No!" shouted Castus, putting his hands over his ears. "This is madness, Lucius! Ever since Olivia died, in that earthquake, you have been saying these crazy things. Her death was tragic, but it was the will of the gods! The gods rule us, and the priests are the only ones who can speak to the gods. They will appease Vulcan and stop this."

"Please, Castus! I beg you! Come with me and Marcus. Let's leave this city," said my father. "I tell you, Pompeii will be destroyed and everyone in it will die!"

I could see that my uncle was trembling with anger. He pointed at the door to the street.

"Get out!" he shouted. "I will not have you coming here and scaring my family this way. You may be my brother, but I will not allow it!"

"Very well!" retorted my father. "If you won't let me save you, perhaps there are others who will listen to me. Come, Marcus!"

With that my father ran out of the house, just as another tremor shook it, making ornaments and vases fall off the shelves and tables and crash to the floor.

I heard Fabius and Julia yelp in fear, and Aunt Drusilla making comforting noises. I looked at my uncle and gave a shrug of apology.

"I'm sorry, Uncle," I said. "I'll try and talk to him. I wish he would listen to you, but you know he doesn't listen to anyone. I'd better go and look after him."

I ran out of the house, not sure where my father would have gone. Then I remembered what my aunt had said: a sacrifice of chickens was being made in the square. If that's where everyone was, that's where I'd find my father – he'd want a big audience.

I hurried to the square in Pompeii and saw eight priests, standing in a circle, offering loud prayers to the god, Vulcan. Next to them was a pile of wooden crates, each with squawking chickens inside. Standing by the crates was a soldier with a knife in his hand. A crowd had gathered round the priests.

Then I saw my father. He was climbing up on a plinth. A statue had fallen off the plinth and lay broken beside it.

To my horror, he began to shout at the priests and the people.

"People of Pompeii, listen to me! This earthquake is nothing to do with Vulcan. Vulcan does not exist!" As the people turned away from the priests and looked towards my father, horrified by his words, he pointed towards the mountain, Vesuvius.

"This earthquake is caused by the fires raging under Vesuvius. There is nothing you, or the priests, can do about it. Vesuvius will explode. And when it does it will shower this city with hot ash. Rivers of fire will pour down from the mountain. You will all die unless you leave now and get to higher ground away from the mountain. Flee!"

There were loud shouts of anger from the crowd, as they began throwing rocks at my father and shouting: "Silence him! It is his fault! He insulted Vulcan!"

The rocks hit my father and he fell backwards onto the cobbles. I ran to help him up, as others also rushed towards him, some arming themselves with wooden sticks.

My father scrambled to his feet, grabbed me by the hand, and dragged me into a side street. He was bleeding from a gash in his head where a stone had hit him.

"We have to make people see the truth, Marcus!" he panted. "We have to save them!"

"No!" I shouted at him. And now I felt tears stinging my eyes. "They're right! This earthquake is all your fault. You have insulted Vulcan! I hate you! I hate you!"

And with that, I ran away from him as fast as I could.

CHAPTER

I headed towards my uncle's house, but the earthquakes were getting more violent and it was hard to walk. Buildings were shaking and cracks were appearing in their walls. With another shake the cracks would suddenly get bigger. Whole sections of wall would fall away into the street, causing the building to come crashing down. Everywhere I went I could hear screams.

It was impossible to move fast. I had to watch all the time, that each building I was passing wasn't about to fall on top of me.

My progress was made harder by the dust that flew into the air whenever a building collapsed, creating a thick choking cloud that filled the street.

I headed for the richer part of the city where the buildings were better built, stronger and not so close together to try to get to my uncle's house that way. It would take longer, but it was safer.

The cloud that had brought the warm flakes from Vesuvius now rained stones upon our heads. They were pumice stones, so they were lighter than normal stones, but some were as big as melons so they still hurt when they hit. At first this rain of pumice stones was light, but it got heavier. The stones made walking difficult because, in the thick clouds of dust, it was hard to see where they were, and I kept tripping and stumbling.

Most of the fountains had split open and water was gushing out. As I passed one, the water splashed me and with a shock I realized it was hot! It also stank of rotten eggs. Why? Was this the work of Vulcan, or was it being heated by the fires underground, just like my father said? If my father was right, then the priests and everyone else were wrong. It was too confusing – could the priests really be wrong?

I tore the bottom part of my tunic off and dipped it in water. I tied it around the lower part of my head to cover my mouth and nose and stop the dust from choking me.

Slowly, slowly, I made my way back to my uncle's house. The air seemed to have cleared a bit here, although the lumps of warm pumice were still raining down. As I got closer, I saw Uncle Castus and Aunt Drusilla hurry Fabius and Julia out into the street, then go back inside to get their belongings. Then, it happened so suddenly, there was a huge tremor and the whole street beneath my feet seemed to lift up, the cobbles shooting upwards. As I fell I saw a massive crack appear in my uncle's house; and the next second, before I could shout a warning, the roof crashed down and the whole house disappeared in a cloud of thick smoke.

CHAPTER

I stood there, horrified, frozen to the spot. I felt sick. What had happened? Were they dead? Surely no one could survive the roof falling down on them like that.

A huge part of me wanted to run away, but I knew I couldn't just leave them. I ran into the cloud of orange dust and smoke. Fabius and Julia were by what remained of the front of the house, clinging to one another, terrified and crying.

"Stay here!" I told them.

The dust had begun to settle and I could see the

ruin of the house – it was just a pile of broken bricks and roof tiles. My heart was pounding as I edged forward through the broken wall. What would I find? Was there any way they could have survived? My uncle and aunt were lying half-buried beneath the rubble. I ran to them and began pulling bricks off them. They weren't moving.

Uncle Castus's arms and feet were sticking out. As I lifted away the bricks, which were covering his head, I realized he was dead. The falling roof must have killed him instantly.

I went to Aunt Drusilla. The bricks and roof tiles had landed on her too, crushing her. She was also dead.

I looked at them, feeling stunned and sick. These were people I'd known all my life, my family, and their lives had been ended in a matter of seconds. What on earth could I say to Fabius and Julia?

Another tremor shook the ground, making me lose my balance and fall. I knew we couldn't stay here. It was too dangerous. With my father gone, and my uncle and aunt dead, I would have to be the grown-up.

I went back outside to where Fabius and Julia were standing, holding one another and crying.

"I'm afraid your mother and father are dead," I told them.

It was brutal. I should have said it better, but there was no time to lose if we were going to get away to safety.

At my words both of them let out howls that were awful to hear, making me feel even more guilty about the way I'd told them. I knelt down, wrapped my arms around them and hugged them tightly.

"You can cry later," I told them. "Right now, we have to get away."

The shaking had stopped, but for how long?

The flakes and lumps of pumice that had been coming down were now joined by a sleet of warm ash that was falling on the city. It must be coming from the thick clouds that were gushing up from the volcano. The ash was starting to pile up on the ground like thick snow, and it was getting thicker all the time.

I stood, holding the twins by their hands, and wondered what to do next. I didn't want to leave the bodies of my uncle and aunt where they were, but I didn't know what else to do. The bricks and rubble covering them would take too long to move, and even if I managed it, what would I do next? Everyone was running around in a panic. No one would help me take the bodies to a proper place. I knew we couldn't stay here. We had to get to safety.

My father had talked about getting to higher ground, but would that be any safer? Then a thought struck me: perhaps if we went to higher ground, we might find my father and he would take care of us.

As we stood there a crowd of people came past us, battling their way through the piles of fallen ash that clogged up the streets.

"Where are you going?" I called out to them.

"To the docks!" one man shouted back. "We're going to get boats to safety!"

Of course! The sea!

"Come on!" I told Fabius and Julia. "Follow me! We're heading for the boats."

I joined the crowd and half-led, half-dragged the twins along with me. Even though the ground had stopped shaking, walking was difficult because of all the rubble lying around from the fallen buildings, and the ever-increasing ash. Trying to walk through the ash was harder than walking through snow, it was like walking through sand.

"Keep going!" I urged Fabius and Julia.

Finally, we reached the docks. It was an incredible sight. There were hundreds and hundreds of people crammed together, all fighting to board the boats tied up at the quayside. But the most amazing thing was the sea. Instead of it stretching away, blue in colour like usual, lumps of pumice of all sizes bobbed about on its surface. As I watched, more lumps of pumice rained down from the sky, and some with smoke and fire trailing behind them.

Some of these fiery rocks landed on the boats, setting light to the wood and the sails. What were we going to do? Even if we did manage to get on a boat, it might catch fire!

Suddenly I heard a shout close by.

"That boy was with the man who caused this! The man who insulted Vulcan!"

I turned and saw a man pointing angrily at me.

"It's his fault!" the man yelled. "Don't let him on the boats or Vulcan will strike that boat with fire!"

A crowd was gathering to see what the commotion was.

"Kill him!" shouted someone else. "Show Vulcan we are sorry! Kill the boy!"

CHAPTER

6

Without pausing to think, I grabbed Julia and Fabius and ran. From the looks of terror and anger on the people's faces, I knew it was a waste of time trying to tell them it wasn't my fault, that I didn't agree with what my father had said about Vulcan. I ducked into a narrow side alley and kept running. It was hard going because of the deep layers of ash. Fabius and Julia fell over a couple of times, but I tugged at their hands and shouted at them to get up and run. All the time I was glancing over my shoulder expecting to see people chasing after me.

Finally, I pulled to a halt beside a ruined building and looked back. No one had followed us. I guessed that they were more worried about getting on one of the boats and escaping.

"What are we going to do?" asked Julia, looking at me, terror showing on her face.

"We'll go to Herculaneum," I said.

It was an instant decision, a reaction to the crowds chasing us. I still wanted to find my father, but now I knew we couldn't stay here in Pompeii in case someone else recognized me.

Herculaneum was the next city along the coast and, like Pompeii, had a port with lots of boats. The people there wouldn't know me or my father. We might be able to board a boat there.

"How will we get there?" asked Fabius.

"We'll walk," I said.

"But it's miles!"

That was true. Herculaneum was about eight miles away. But I was trying to stay positive for the children.

"There are villages on the way," I told them. "Villages with fishermen. We might get lucky and find someone with a boat who'll take us to safety. And we'll be safer out on a country road that we are in the city. There won't be any buildings or statues to fall on us."

As I said the words, I knew I'd said the wrong thing. I could see the eyes of both Fabius and Julia fill up with tears as they thought of their house falling down on their parents.

"I'm sorry," I said. "I didn't mean to upset you. Please, I know it's hard for you, but try not to think about it for now. We need to focus on getting to safety."

It felt strange, me giving orders. I was used to being told what to do by adults. But now, at twelve years old, I found myself in charge of my young cousins, because it didn't look like anyone was going to help us.

We headed away from the docks and made for the coast road to Herculaneum. Walking was still difficult, and I quickly realized it would take us longer than normal to get to Herculaneum, but we didn't have much choice. Normally it would take about three hours to walk from Pompeii, but with this ash slowing us down, it might take four times as long. But we couldn't stay at the docks, and if we stayed in Pompeii we would be in danger from collapsing buildings if there were any more shocks or tremors.

By now it was early evening and dusk was falling. Not that it made much difference – it had seemed like dusk all that afternoon because of the dark clouds from Vesuvius that still hung over Pompeii.

We weren't the only people trying to escape along the coast road to Herculaneum. Lots of empty carts had been abandoned on the road. The thick piles of ash and the pumice that had been thrown out from the volcano made travelling by cart almost impossible. There were also big cracks in the road, and the wheels of some of the carts had sunk into them. People had unhitched the horses from their carts, piled as much as they could onto their backs, and travelled on. But even the horses were having difficulty, struggling along in these terrible conditions.

The situation was made worse because there were

lots of people coming from Herculaneum towards Pompeii, so I guessed things were just as bad there. I began to wonder if it was such a good idea us heading for Herculaneum after all. The coast road was jammed with people, which made travelling even harder.

"We need to get off this road," I told the twins. I pointed to where the fields went up into the hills inland. "We'll go across country."

"It's getting dark," said Fabius, worried. "There are wolves out there!"

The same fearful thought had occurred to me. But then I remembered the dead sheep my father and I had seen when we first arrived on the outskirts of Pompeii.

"The bad smell coming from the mountain has frightened the wild animals away," I assured him.

I didn't know if that was true, but I knew I had to persuade them to leave the road, otherwise we'd never get to Herculaneum.

As we left the mass of people struggling along the road and began to climb the hill, I thought of the other dangers we might encounter. Wolves. Bears.

Wild dogs. I thought of my father. Was he still alive? Was he somewhere looking for safety like us?

I gripped Fabius and Julia tightly by their hands.

"You'll be alright," I promised them. "I'll look after you."

CHAPTER

We climbed up the hill and came to an olive grove. Here the ash that had fallen wasn't lying as thick on the ground as in the city, so we set off between the trees, still heading north towards Herculaneum. I kept us walking at the very edge of the olive grove because I was worried that there might be dangerous wild animals hiding among the trees, but there didn't seem to be any about. I remembered that my father had once told me, that when there was going to be an earthquake or a big storm, all the wild animals and birds feel it before people do, and leave the area. If he was right, we should be safe. But then my father had also said things that I thought were crazy. Like when he said there were no gods. If there were no gods, then where did everything come from? The sky, the land and trees, the oceans and rivers – someone had to make them.

Because the ground was uneven, I let Julia and Fabius walk on their own, so they could keep their balance. But suddenly Julia tripped and fell. She half-rolled and half-slid down the hill, and the next second she had disappeared!

"Julia!" shouted Fabius in alarm.

He and I ran to where she'd disappeared, and saw that an enormous hole had opened up in the ground and she'd tumbled into it. There was a dreadful smell coming up from the hole, the same smell there had been in the fields of dead sheep. The air coming up from the hole was hot.

Even though it was getting dark, I could see that Julia had landed on something big and bulky in the hole, which had stopped her falling any further.

She was about two metres below the ground, and the thing she'd landed on looked as if it was rocking.

"Are you alright?" I called down to her.

"I've hurt my leg!" she called back, tearfully. "I think I twisted my ankle!"

"What are you lying on?" I shouted.

"It's a broken cart," she called back. "It's wobbling! I think it's going to fall!"

"Stay there and keep as still as you can!" I told her. "I'll come down and get you!"

I looked into the hole. Even in the dim light of dusk I could see that the sides of the hole were steep. There didn't seem to be any places I could use as handholds or footholds.

I wished there was someone who could help us – an adult. Someone big and strong. But there wasn't. It was down to me.

I looked around, wondering what I could use to save Julia. And then I had an idea.

"I need your tunic," I told Fabius.

"Why?" he asked.

"Because I'm going to make a rope."

I took off my own short robe and tore strips off it. Then I tore Fabius's tunic into strips and tied them all together to make one long rope. I tied one end to the thick branch of an olive tree, then dropped the other end down to Julia.

"Can you get hold of that and climb up?" I asked.

"No!" Julia shouted back. I could hear the fear in her voice. "The cart is really wobbling. If I move, it'll fall down even more! And I don't know how deep the hole is! I think it goes right down into the Underworld!"

"Don't panic. Stay there and I'll come and get you!" I called.

I tested the rope by pulling at it. It seemed to be strong enough, but I didn't know if it would take my weight.

"I'll hang on to it," offered Fabius.

I shook my head.

"No. If the rope breaks and you're hanging on to it, you'll be pulled down with us. And, like Julia says, we don't know how deep down the hole is." I went to the edge of the hole and took hold of my homemade rope. "Fabius, listen to me. If it goes wrong and we both end up in the hole, go back to the road and follow the crowd. Head for the sea. Someone will find a place for you in a boat."

Fabius suddenly grabbed me and hugged me, looking terrified.

"I don't want to be left alone without you and Julia!" He began to cry.

"I don't want that, either," I told him. "But I have to try to save Julia."

I eased myself out of his arms as gently as I could and then began to climb carefully down the rope. The smell in the hole was awful, the same stink as before, but the heat coming up from below made it even worse. It was as if I was actually climbing down into Vulcan's forge, deep below the ground. I had no idea if I would be able to reach Julia and get us both back to the surface again.

CHAPTER

I climbed down slowly, all the time aware that the rope was only made of cloth and it might tear at any moment. If that happened I knew I'd fall on top of Julia and take her, and the cart, right down to the depths.

At last, I made it to where Julia was sitting on the broken remains of a cart. It was certainly rocking. I saw that it was balanced on a rock that was jutting out. If it slipped off that rock it would fall much further into the hole. The pit was so deep I couldn't see the bottom. And the smell coming up from it was really horrible – so bad it made my eyes water.

"Can you slide towards me and grab my hand?" I asked.

"I'm scared!" shouted Julia.

I braced my feet against the side of the hole and, holding on to the rope with one hand, stretched out my other hand as far as I could.

"Come on!" I urged her. "Hold my hand!"

Nervously, Julia reached out. I reached further until our fingers were almost touching.

"Make one last stretch," I said. "Come on, Julia."

As she stretched a bit more, so did I, and I was able to get my fingers round her wrist. Suddenly I saw the cart shift and then edge off the rock it was balanced on. I tightened my grip on her wrist and pulled her to me just as the cart fell away. As it did, I saw that the body of a woman had been caught beneath the cart, and she went down with it, her dress fluttering in the gloom as she, and the cart, disappeared into the darkness below.

Another dead person. This was becoming an even worse nightmare. I hoped that Julia hadn't seen her.

"Hang on tightly!" I shouted.

I pulled Julia to me.

"Put your arms around my neck!" I yelled.

One of Julia's arms grabbed me round my neck. She clung on tightly to my wrist with her other hand.

"Use both arms!" I shouted at her.

"I'm scared of letting go of your hand!" she shouted back, terrified. She was shaking with fear.

"I need both my hands to climb back up!" I said urgently. "Come on, Julia! Do this and we'll be alright, I promise!"

Julia hesitated, then she let go of my wrist and made a lunge for my neck, and then she was clinging to me.

Despite what I'd told her about us being alright, I was terrified that our weight would be too much for the rope and it would tear. If that happened, there would be nothing to stop us falling.

Very slowly, and sick with fear, I hauled us up the rope, hand over hand, bracing my feet against the earth wall. As we neared the top, I shouted, "Fabius! Come and grab your sister!"

Fabius reached down and took hold of Julia by her

dress, taking her weight off me a bit, while I climbed right to the top of the hole.

I clambered out, with Julia still clinging to me, and we both collapsed on the ground.

I crawled towards the olive grove, dragging Julia after me. I wanted to get us away from the edge of the hole as fast as we could. Only when I was sure that we were safe in the cover of the trees did I let her go. There may be wolves here, but I'd rather risk a wolf than go near that dreadful hole again.

I lay on the ground, gasping for my breath, my heart pounding.

"It's too dangerous for us to keep walking in the dark," I told the twins. "There might be other holes we could fall into. We'll stay here until it gets light. Then we'll be able to see where we're going."

"I'm hungry," said Fabius.

I nodded. So was I. It was now night-time, and I hadn't eaten anything since early that morning.

I pointed at the olive trees.

"Take some olives. They'll be hard chewing, but they'll help ease your appetite. And there's oil in them."

As Fabius went to the nearest olive tree and began

searching among the leaves for fruits, Julia said: "I'm too scared to eat." She let out a whimper of pain. "And my ankle hurts."

"We'll rest," I told her. "Hopefully, it might feel better in the morning."

But I knew it wouldn't. Once, when I'd twisted my ankle, it had swollen so badly I couldn't walk. Tomorrow, when daylight came, Julia would have to be carried.

CHAPTER

As the night wore on, I sat with my back against the trunk of one of the olive trees and watched Julia and Fabius as they slept. I held a broken piece of branch in my hands in case any wild animals should come sniffing around. It wouldn't be much of a weapon, but my hope was that it might keep them at bay. I'd also gathered a few rocks by my side, ready to throw at any animals that came close.

But so far there had been no sight or sound of anything or anyone. No wolves howling. No wild dogs barking. I wondered if my father had been right about animals sensing when something bad was about to happen, like an earthquake.

Vesuvius had actually settled down now. There was still the odd rumble and a slight shake of the ground, but nothing as bad as there had been before. The flakes and rocks had also stopped raining down. I wondered if the danger was passed. Was Vulcan happier now? It struck me that maybe my father had been killed, and that was why Vulcan wasn't feeling as angry. Tears sprang to my eyes at the thought.

Please, Vulcan don't let him be dead! I prayed. I didn't want my last words to my father to be that I hated him. I didn't hate him. I had just been so angry and scared.

I wished I could see him again, to tell him that I missed him. I wanted us to be back together.

In the distance I could see red, flickering glows from Vesuvius, lighting up the night sky.

In the morning, I'd take Fabius and Julia to Herculaneum. We'd find a boat and get to safety by sea until the earthquake and the volcano stopped. And then I'd try and find my father.

*

It was the rumbling and shaking that woke me up. I must have fallen asleep, even though I'd tried to stay awake to keep guard. The events of the day had exhausted me.

The noise was coming from Vesuvius. I stood up so I could get a better view of the mountain. The red glow that had been coming from it before was now much brighter. It looked as if the top of the mountain was actually bubbling red. Then, as I watched, the top of the mountain seemed to collapse – red burst out of it and began to run down the side of the mountain like a river of fire. Not a narrow stream, but a wide, fast-flowing river, travelling as quickly as any river made of water. I'd never seen anything like it before. I couldn't make sense of what I was seeing, but I knew something was terribly wrong.

In the distance, I could see the lights of Herculaneum glowing softly, and it looked as if the river of fire was heading straight towards the city.

Even in the darkness, I could see thick smoke surging upwards as the river of fire raced down the mountain, burning everything in its path, all the time getting nearer and nearer to the lights of

Herculaneum. With horror I thought of the hundreds of people we'd seen heading towards the city and how we would have been there too, if Julia hadn't fallen down the hole. All of those people were trapped in the city. Even if they tried to run, the river of fire was moving at such a speed they would never get out in time.

I wanted to close my eyes, to shut out the horror, but I couldn't. I was held spellbound by the sight of that enormous, heaving mass of burning liquid as it got nearer and nearer to the city.

And then it struck. I thought I heard screams, even from this distance, but it could have been my imagination. The huge river of fire burst over Herculaneum, devouring the whole city and every living thing in it.

CHAPTER

10

I stood there in shock. I had just seen a whole city destroyed and everyone in it killed in the space of a few minutes. I was shaking, and I sat down heavily, my mind whirling. What should we do? Would we be next? Should we run? But where to?

Again, I wished someone older was here to guide us and tell us what to do. My father, or my uncle and aunt. But they weren't here. No-one was here. It was just me, Fabius and Julia.

Think! I told myself. The river of fire had flowed

down the side of the volcano to Herculaneum. We were on higher ground than the city, but we were still below the top of Vesuvius.

In the red glow from the volcano that lit up the sky, I scanned the land ahead. I was searching to see if there were any valleys, but there didn't seem to be. So, if another river of fire poured out of the volcano and came in *our* direction, heading towards Pompeii, there were no valleys for it to run down; it would come straight for us.

We needed to get to higher ground and away from the mountain – and quickly!

I shook Fabius and Julia awake.

"What is it?" asked Fabius. "Is it day yet?"

"No," I told him. "But we have to move."

Julia began to get up, but then she screamed in pain and fell down.

"My ankle!" she cried.

"I'll carry you," I said.

"Why can't we wait till daylight?" asked Fabius.

"Because the mountain has exploded and sent a river of fire down towards the sea. It's already destroyed Herculaneum," I told them, bluntly.

They stared at me, their mouths and eyes open in shock.

"Destroyed Herculaneum?" repeated Fabius, his voice a terrified whisper.

"The whole town," I said, sadly. "I didn't want to tell you, but I had to. You need to know the danger we're in if we stay here."

"If the volcano explodes again and the river of fire heads towards Pompeii, we'll be right in the way. We have to get to higher ground."

Fabius and Julia looked at one another in horror as the realization dawned on them.

"But you said walking in the dark was dangerous. The last time we walked in the dark, Julia fell down that hole. You said it was safer to wait until daylight," Fabius said.

"Yes, but we don't know when the mountain might blow up again." I pointed at the olive trees. "We'll go up through the olive grove, going from tree to tree. That way we should be safe."

I knelt down beside Julia and let her climb on to my back. Then I stood up so that she was hanging on my back like a sack. Luckily she was fairly light.

"Right. Follow me and watch where you step," I told Fabius.

We headed up the hill through the olive grove. Although it was still night-time the sky glowed red, which helped us see where we were going. A hot wind blew sparks from Herculaneum below and Vesuvius above, which fluttered down around us, now and then touching us and burning our bare skin.

"It hurts," moaned Fabius.

I began to wish I'd kept our torn tunics to make some kind of cover for us to wear out of them, but I knew it wouldn't have worked.

"Just grit your teeth and try and think of other things," I said. "Think of cool, fresh rain."

"That's stupid," said Fabius.

Fortunately the olive trees gave us some kind of cover from the falling sparks.

We carried on climbing up the hill. The further we went, the heavier Julia seemed to become. All the time I kept shooting looks towards Vesuvius, dreading another river of fire. The top of the volcano looked like it was bubbling red-hot. The river of fire, that had run down its side to Herculaneum, still glowed and a strong stench of burning was blown towards us on the warm wind.

We were nearing the far end of the olive grove, when suddenly, we heard what sounded like a howl.

"Wolves!" cried Fabius, frightened.

We stood stock still, peering into the darkness. Then we heard the sound again. But it wasn't wolves.

It was a baby crying.

CHAPTER

I peered in the direction where the sound came from and saw a small wooden barn near the edge of the olive grove.

"It's coming from over there," I said. "Let's go. Be careful where you walk."

Fabius followed me as I carried Julia towards the barn. The nearer we got, the louder the baby's cries.

When we got there, I put Julia down on the ground then cautiously opened the barn door.

" Mummy, is that you?" I heard a young child ask.

"No," I said. "My name's Marcus. Who's in there?"

I saw that there were three young children and a baby huddled together.

Just then, there was another explosion from the volcano – there was the same deep rumbling sound as before, then a violent shaking and the sky lit up with a tremendous light.

I turned to look at Vesuvius. I was hardly able to breathe for fear that this latest explosion would mean a river of fire was on its way towards us. But, although the top of the mountain bubbled with red like before, the fire seemed to be staying inside the volcano's crater, for now.

"You have to leave," I told the children. "It's too dangerous to stay here."

"We can't," said one. "We have to wait here for our parents. That's what they told us."

"Where are they?" I asked.

"Our father went to Herculaneum." The speaker was a boy of about eight.

"Then our mother went to get him," added a girl of about six. "She went in our cart. She told us to stay here, said we'd be safer in the barn than in our house."

"How long ago did she go?" I asked.

There was an unhappy silence, then the girl replied: "I'm not sure. A long time ago. Before it got dark."

I remembered the broken cart we'd found in the hole, and the body of the woman I'd seen falling down into the chasm, and realized that it was quite likely their mother. She must have been driving the cart alongside the olive grove when the ground opened up and swallowed the cart, the horse and her.

"I'm really sorry but don't think they're coming back," I told the children.

"But they said they would!" burst out the smallest child. "Mummy promised us!"

"Bad things are happening because of the mountain," I said. I hesitated, then added: "I think they're dead." I had to tell them the truth if I was going to persuade them to leave.

"No!" the girl shouted at me.

"Yes," I said, sadly. "Herculaneum has been destroyed by a river of fire that poured out of Vesuvius. I saw it happening."

"It doesn't mean that our father is dead!" insisted the girl. "He might have got away!"

"He might," I nodded.

"And Mummy might come back."

I shook my head.

"I think we found her and your cart in a hole near the olive grove. The ground opened up and swallowed them."

The children looked at me in horror, and then the girl and the youngest child, a boy, began to cry. I saw the lips of the eldest tremble as he struggled to stop himself crying too.

"The important thing is we have to get you all to a safe place," I said. "If your father is alive, he'll find you later."

But I knew that wouldn't happen. If he'd been in Herculaneum then he was dead. No one could have survived that river of fire.

"Do you have any other animals?" I asked.

"We have a donkey," said the boy.

"Good." I pointed towards Fabius and Julia sitting outside, waiting. "My cousin has hurt her leg and can't walk. She can ride on the donkey and hold the baby. What's his name?"

"Minerva," said the girl crossly. "She's a girl, not a boy."

"Sorry," I apologized. Another thought struck me. "We also need some clothes. And food and water."

"There's some at the house," said the oldest boy. Deciding that he was going to trust me, he introduced himself and the others: "I'm Leontes. That's my sister Popilla and my brother Claudius. Minerva's our baby sister. She's only a year old."

"My name's Marcus," I told him in return. "The two outside are my cousins, Fabius and Julia." Then I added, hoping it might make them feel less alone, "Their parents, my uncle and aunt, died yesterday in Pompeii. Their house collapsed on them. My father has disappeared, too, Everywhere is dangerous. Your mother was right to make you stay in this barn."

CHAPTER

12

I followed Leontes and Popilla to their house to get provisions as well as some clothes for myself and Fabius, while Fabius stayed to look after Julia, Claudius and the baby. I learned that Leontes was eight years old. Popilla was five and Claudius was four. As I was twelve and the oldest, I was in charge, although some of the scowling looks that Popilla threw at me told me that she didn't trust me completely. I could understand that. If I'd been her, I wouldn't have trusted some twelve-year-old who turned up and started giving orders, especially if they included ordering me out of my house. Luckily, Leontes seemed to accept me.

By the time we were ready to leave, it was getting light. Leontes had given Fabius and me some of his clothes to put on, and Popilla had filled leather bags with water from the animals' drinking trough. The water in their own cistern tasted and smelt as foul as the water in Pompeii.

We put Julia on their donkey, which was called Acorn, and gave her the baby, Minerva, to hold. Leontes led the donkey by its rope halter, and the rest of us walked alongside.

"Where are we going?" asked Popilla suspiciously. "We should be heading down to Pompeii. That's where people are. That's where we'll be safest."

"Pompeii is below the mountain and there's a valley from Vesuvius that runs right down to it. If another river of fire comes from the volcano, it might run down the valley and cover the city. Just like what happened at Herculaneum."

"But there are boats in Pompeii," insisted Popilla. "We could get away over the sea."

Suddenly, Leontes stopped.

"Look!" he said.

We looked to where he was pointing.

From where we stood, high on the hill, we could see the city of Pompeii below us. Even from this distance we could see that many of the buildings had collapsed and were just broken ruins, though most of the houses in the richer areas seemed to still be standing.

There was a lot of activity in the city. I expected it was people trying to clear up after the earthquake. But what Leontes was actually pointing to was the sea beyond Pompeii. The surface of the water was covered with floating rocks of all sizes. The way they bobbed about on the water showed they were made of pumice. But the horrifying thing was the wrecked boats trapped among them – smoke coming from many of them. It looked like the rain of hot pumice falling on the bay had set fire to many of the boats. I could only imagine how it must have felt for the people who'd managed to get on board a boat and cast off for safety, only for the boat to catch fire. There would have been no way back to the shore for them, so they would either have drowned or burnt to death. Surely some of the boats must have got away. I wondered how many of the people I'd seen at the port yesterday had managed to escape to safety.

"There's no way we can catch a boat now," said Leontes.

"We'll carry on across country until we get to a road. If I'm right, that'll be the road my father and I came in on yesterday. That road will take us out of here and back to my village. We'll be safe there. There are deep valleys and gulleys between my village and the volcano. If the mountain explodes again and another river of fire pours out, they'll stop it."

"How far is it?" asked Popilla.

"It's a long way," said Fabius. "Remember, Marcus, when we came to visit you and your father, and it took us half a day? And that was travelling by horse and cart."

"We'll take it in stages," I said. "The main thing is we have to get on a high road that takes us away from Pompeii."

"The volcano seems to have settled down," said Leontes.

"We ought to go back home then," said Popilla. "In case Daddy comes back."

"He isn't coming back!" I said. "If he was in Herculaneum he's dead!"

"You don't know that!" shouted Popilla. "He may not have got as far as Herculaneum! He may be heading for home now!" She glared at me. "I don't care what you say. You're just trying to scare us. I'm going back home!" She looked at elder brother. "Come on, Leontes. Acorn is our donkey. We're going home with him."

As she said this, there was a terrible rumble from the mountain. The ground shook so hard beneath our feet that we all fell over. The donkey stumbled and I thought Julia was going to fall off, or at least drop the baby, but she managed to hold on to little Minerva with one arm and the donkey's mane with her other hand.

As I pushed myself up off the ground, I looked towards Vesuvius and a feeling of terror welled up in me, making it hard to breathe. The top of the mountain had blown up again, and another river of fire was pouring out. It was heading straight towards us!

CHAPTER

13

"Run!" I screamed.

I leapt to my feet and ran to Acorn. I grabbed hold of the rope around its neck and began to pull, desperately shouting at the donkey to move, but it stayed stubbornly where it was.

The others had also got up and turned, and now saw the river of fire pouring out of the mountain and heading for us.

Leontes ran to the donkey. He snatched the rope

from my hand, said something to the donkey, and it began to move. He said something else, and the donkey began to trot.

"Hold on tight!" I shouted at Julia.

Popilla ran to the donkey, reaching up her arms.

"Give me Minerva!" she shouted. "I can run with her!"

Julia hesitated, then passed the baby down to Popilla, who grabbed her baby sister up in her arms.

"Where are we going?" screamed Popilla at me.

I pointed up the hill.

"Higher!" I yelled.

We were all running now, not caring if stones or holes might trip us up. We were only aware of the burning river of fire bearing down towards us. I could feel the heat of it on my back getting more intense; hear the cracking sounds and small explosions as it got nearer and nearer. I could hear sudden violent crashes as trees and bushes burst into flames. The smell of burning wood, leaves and grass filled my nostrils.

A few times I stumbled and nearly fell, but fear of what was behind us kept me going, as did the need to make sure I kept the others safe. I kept casting glances around to make sure that they were still running. They were, but their eyes and mouths were wide open with terror.

Suddenly the terrible rumbling sound seemed to die down. There were still explosions and cracking sounds, but they seemed a little more distant than before. We kept running.

Throwing a frantic look over my shoulder, I saw that the river of fire seemed to have stopped, almost as if it had run out of speed. Still terrified and not quite trusting it, I carried on running with the others. Then little Claudius stumbled and fell, crashing to the ground.

I ran to pick him up, and this time when I looked back I saw that the river of fire had slid to a halt barely a quarter of a mile away from us.

"It's stopped!" I shouted.

The others turned, and saw that the huge, heaving river of burning red fire had stopped, although it was still dangerously close.

None of us could take our eyes off the burning river. My father had told me the real name for it was lava, and that it was made of rocks that had melted in the heat and become liquid. When the lava cooled, it would turn into rock again.

I could see that this was already starting to happen. The massive, burning red river was starting to turn grey in places. It was like looking at the biggest fire there had ever been, but with rocks blazing instead of hot coals. Even from this distance we could feel the heat coming from it. Every so often a movement in the earth caused a crack to open – smoke and red liquid poured out and set fire to the grass.

Popilla looked back towards her house and tears began to roll down her face. Where their house and barn and olive grove had been, there was now just a solid mass of burning rocks.

"It's all gone!" she cried. "If Daddy did come back. . ."

Leontes went to her and hugged her close.

"We have to go on, Popilla," he said.

"And quickly," I urged them. "It's stopped for the moment, but it could start moving again." I went to the sobbing Popilla and wrapped my arms around her and Leontes. "I'm sorry, Popilla. But the harsh truth is that all we have now is one another. We're still alive. And your parents would want you to do everything you could to stay alive. I know you don't like me, and you don't think I know what I'm doing. But if I hadn't made you to leave your barn, you'd all be dead now. Trust me, and I'll do my best to get us all to safety."

She nodded and wiped her eyes with her hand.

I looked again at the smouldering lava. At the nearest point to us it had trickled down to a thin layer of grey rock, but further back it was as high as a person. And it still glowed red beneath the grey. As it cooled it moved, almost as if it was breathing. It looked as if it was alive.

All around the lava, wherever it had touched, there were flames. It had set light to the grass and trees and bushes, and the air was filled with a terrible stench of burning. I shuddered at the sickening realisation that if we hadn't run, that smell of burning would have been us.

"Come on," I said. "Keep going."

CHAPTER

14

Claudius had hurt his knee when he'd fallen and couldn't move very fast, so we put him on the donkey along with Julia. Popilla insisted on carrying Minerva. We were just about to set off when Fabius suddenly threw up.

"I'm sorry," he apologised, wiping his mouth. "Thinking of what nearly happened to us made me feel sick."

"Me too," I told him.

With Leontes leading the donkey, we carried on

up the hill towards where I hoped the road might be. All the time, all of us were sickeningly aware of how close we'd been to being killed by the river of fire, and terrified that there might be another surge of lava from the mountain. The smell of burning stayed with us as we walked.

What I couldn't get over was how fast the lava had moved. It really had seemed more like water than rock, like a fast-flowing river.

Below us we could see the people of Pompeii still clearing up after the earthquakes. I wondered if they realized how close they'd come to being wiped out. If the river of fire had carried on down the mountainside, it was on a direct course for the city and would have covered it in red-hot lava, just as had happened with Herculaneum.

"There's a road ahead!" shouted Leontes.

Yes, there it was not far away. As we drew nearer to it, I recognized the wreckage of our cart with the dead body of our poor old horse, Pallas, lying beside it.

"That's our cart!" I told them. "This is the road we want!"

We quickened our pace, but as we moved closer

I stopped. Someone was there, stepping out from behind the wrecked cart. It was a wild-looking man, naked except for a loincloth and covered with ash and soot. In his hand he clutched a long sword.

CHAPTER

15

"Marcus! Is that you!"

I stared at the man, stunned. I recognized his voice. It was my father!

"It's Uncle Lucius!" shouted Fabius, and he and I both broke into a run towards him.

My father threw the sword onto the cart and ran towards us, his arms open wide. I threw myself into them.

"I thought you were dead!" I said, tears rolling down my face as I hugged him tightly.

"I thought you were dead!" he replied.

He looked at Fabius, his face suddenly sad.

"Where are your parents?" he asked.

I saw Fabius's lip tremble and tears come into his eyes. I knew he was too upset to say the words.

"They are both dead," I told my father, standing back from him and wiping my eyes. I gestured towards the others who had joined us now. "This is Leontes, the one leading the donkey, and Popilla, the one holding the baby. The baby's called Minerva. That's their brother, Claudius, on the donkey with Julia. Their parents were also killed. I'm taking them to our house."

My father nodded.

"It's the right thing to do," he agreed. "We all have to help one another."

Curious, I asked him: "Where did the sword come from?"

"I found it," said my father. "So many people were trying to kill me, I decided I needed something to defend myself with. But in the end people were more worried about getting to safety."

Leontes was looking at the broken cart and he asked:

"Is there any way we can mend it? We could tie Acorn to it and he could pull us along. He's very strong."

My father shook his head.

"The axle's broken. We'd need tools to repair it." He pointed at the mountain. "Vesuvius could blow up again at any second. We need to get away from here as quickly as we can and put a valley between us and the volcano so that if it erupts again we won't get caught in the river of lava."

He looked again at the volcano, a worried expression on his face. "The way the lava is bubbling at the top tells me the crater could collapse at any moment. If it does, all the lava inside it will rush out and pour down the mountainside."

"What about the people who are still in Pompeii?" asked Leontes.

"I tried to warn them, but they wouldn't listen to me," said my father sadly. "All we can do is hope they survive."

He went to the cart and picked up the sword.

"Just in case we meet danger on the way," he said.

He set off, heading up the hill. Leontes and Popilla looked at one another, questioningly. Then

Popilla nodded and they set off after him on the road – Popilla carrying Minerva, Julia and Claudius on Acorn. Fabius hurried to catch up with Julia and the donkey.

I turned and looked down on Pompeii – at the ruins, at the people working to try and repair things. I thought of Uncle Castus and Aunt Drusilla lying dead beneath their wrecked house, and how I'd seen a whole city destroyed in minutes when the river of lava had poured down over Herculaneum. I'd survived.

Why had some people died and others lived? Was it the power of the gods? Did the gods decide who lived and who died? If so, why did they choose me and Fabius and Julia to live, and not my uncle and aunt?

Suddenly I heard a deep rumbling sound coming from the direction of Vesuvius. I swung round and saw with horror that this side of the volcano had collapsed, the top of the crater was crumbling and breaking open. There was a bubbling mass of burning fiery red surging out, just as I had seen during the night, only this river of fire looked even bigger and seemed to be moving even faster.

"Marcus!" I heard my father's yell of panic from farther up the road. "Marcus! Run!"

But I couldn't move. I was rooted to the spot, hypnotized by the sight of the enormous river of fire pouring out. It rushed down the side of the mountain, reached the still-smouldering pile of cooling grey lava and overran it, racing over everything in its path.

"Marcus!"

The shout was close to my ear this time. I felt my father's hand grab me roughly and haul me away, dragging me up the road.

We ran. The others were waiting for us at the crest of the hill. The road beyond dipped down to a valley and then rose back up. I realized that if the raging liquid lava came along this road and down into that valley, we would all die. There was no place for us to go where we could escape it.

My father and I joined the others and then turned to gaze in horror at the river of fire as it surged along. As we watched, it swerved away from the road and began following the dips and valleys in the ground, heading down the mountainside straight for Pompeii.

The lava was so near to us that our faces were stung by the heat and smoke.

We watched in horror as the white-hot mass heaved and writhed and poured down on the city.

"Don't look!" shouted my father.

But we couldn't stop ourselves. We stood there, watching a tidal wave of flame and molten rock surging down, wave after wave, hurtling away from us. Even more red-hot lava was pouring out of the mountain now, and rushing after the first surge, then more and more, piling on.

Seen this close, it was wider than the widest river – a huge sea of fire and flame, spreading even further as it flowed. There was no way anyone in the city could escape. The huge burning sea hit the city, then surged on. The buildings disappeared beneath it. Everything disappeared. It covered the whole city and then ran into the sea, cascading out over the water before sinking in a mass of steam and smoke.

Where the great bustling city of Pompeii had been, just moments before, there was now just a sheet of bubbling red lava, turning grey as it cooled in the air.

The city and everything in it had disappeared.

We stood in stunned silence. I realized I was shaking, and when I looked at the others I saw they were shaking, too.

"We are alive," murmured my father. "That is the important thing we must cling to. We are alive."

"We are alive," I repeated, dully, as if trying to force that into my brain.

I began to walk along the road, heading homeward, leaving the scene of utter destruction behind me.

I was aware of the others following me, the clip clop of the donkey's hooves and our footsteps on the road.

We were alive.

The past was buried behind us.

HISTORICAL NOTE

THE DESTRUCTION OF POMPEII

On 5 February AD 62 a serious earthquake almost destroyed Pompeii and the nearby city of Herculaneum. For the next seventeen years the area around Vesuvius suffered from tremors – some large enough to cause deaths, some smaller. On 24 August AD 79, these tremors came to a head when the volcano, Vesuvius, erupted and destroyed the cities of Pompeii and Herculaneum.

The timetable of the eruption

During the morning of 24 August there was a series of shocks and tremors in the area around Vesuvius, gradually getting more and more violent.

At 1 p.m. a large cloud took shape above Vesuvius. Molten ash and pumice were being blown out of the crater at a great rate: about 10,000 tons every second. For the next few hours, lumps of pumice rained down on Pompeii, and layers of it built up on the ground and the roofs of the buildings.

Pumice is less dense than water, so when it landed in the sea it floated.

Volcanic rocks were also being blown out of the volcano by the eruption. These were heavier than pumice, and they smashed through roofs and caused serious injury when they struck people.

By 2.30 p.m. a dark cloud of ash had gathered in the sky over Pompeii, making the sky so dark it was as if dusk had fallen. Layers of pumice and rock were building up on roofs. Buildings were shaking from the constant earth tremors. Over 100,000 tons of rock and ash had already been thrown out by the volcano. The streets of Pompeii were now buried under 50 centimetres of ash. The pumice particles falling on Pompeii were getting bigger, killing more people as they struck.

The thickness of the ash in the streets made walking difficult.

By 6 p.m., with the roofs laden with over 50 centimetres of ash, buildings were collapsing. Many people fled to the shore hoping to be rescued by the Roman navy, but the boats couldn't get to the shore due to the masses of hot pumice floating on the water. Boats moored in Pompeii couldn't get out.

At 8 p.m., magma was now coming from deeper within the volcano. Magma is hotter and heavier and not so rich in gas. This meant that less ash was coming out of Vesuvius. Some people thought the danger was over. They were wrong.

At some time between 1 a.m. and 2 a.m. on 25 August AD 79, part of the crater at the top of Vesuvius collapsed. A river of fire made of lava poured out of the top of the volcano and ran down the side of the mountain heading towards Herculaneum. This avalanche of burning lava travelled at 100 kph and had a temperature of

815°C. When it struck Herculaneum it overran the city and killed everyone.

At 6.30 a.m. there was another surge of lava pouring down from Vesuvius. This one struck Pompeii, killing most of those who had remained in the city. At 7.30 a.m. there was one final outpouring of lava from Vesuvius which travelled at 100 kph. When it hit Pompeii it killed everyone else who was still alive. Pompeii was entombed beneath 6 metres of volcanic rock.

The timetable of discovery

Both cities remained buried beneath thick layers of rock for over 1,500 years. In 1594 an Italian count, Muzio Tuttavilla, started work in the area to build tunnels that would divert water to power grain mills. The workmen uncovered ancient walls with Roman decorations. When wells were dug around Herculaneum in 1706 to try and get new water supplies, the workers uncovered the remains of large buildings. Real investigations to uncover the buried cities began in 1738, and continued through the eighteenth and nineteenth centuries. In the twentieth century, major work was carried out to uncover and preserve the ruins of Pompeii as it looked at the time the lava from the volcano struck the city. The uncovered and preserved cities of Pompeii and Herculaneum are now major tourist attractions.

IF YOU ENJOYED

SURVIVOR
ESCAPE FROM POMPEII

READ ON FOR A TASTE OF

SURVIVOR
TITANIC

CHAPTER

1

"Hey Ralph, can we swap bunks tonight?"

"Why?" My older brother sounded suspicious. "You gonna be kicking my bed springs, Jimmy? Is that it?"

"'Course not, Ralph," I said, trying to sound all innocent. "I just want to try the bottom bunk."

"Fine. But no monkeying around, do you hear me?"

Mam switched out the lights and lay down in her bed next to our bunk bed.

"Sweet dreams, boys," she said. "Only three sleeps

till we reach New York. Three sleeps until we see your pa again and start our new life in America."

The massive engines of the *Titanic* thumped and growled beneath us, and the steady heaving of the ship rocked us to sleep.

At least, it rocked Mam and Ralph. Me, I pinched myself to stay awake. My plans for the night did not include falling asleep.

As soon as it was safe, I slid out of bed and arranged a fake 'Jimmy' under the blankets. I rolled-up clothes for the body and used Ralph's football for the head. Then I crept across the cabin and slipped out, closing the cabin door as quietly as I could.

I climbed the stairs, laughing to myself at the thought of the decoy in my bed and excited by the adventure ahead of me. I had heard stories of the wild parties in the third-class common room at the front of the ship, and now I was going to see one for myself.

The port-side corridor on E deck was the longest corridor in the whole ship. The crew nicknamed it Scotland Road. As I ran along it, the sound of music and laughter grew louder, and when I climbed the last staircase I found myself in the middle of the best party I had ever seen.

A banjo player and an accordion player stood on a table in the middle of the room, playing their instruments hard and fast. The floor around them was filled with men and women clapping and stomping so hard that the whole room shook. I recognized the tune as 'The Little Beggarman', one of the folk songs Pa used to sing when we all lived together back in Kilkenny, before Pa left for America.

I am a little beggarman and begging I have been
For three score years in this little isle of green.

Some of the men and women in the crowd formed lines and began dancing just like they did back home in Ireland. They kept their bodies still but their legs moved like crazy – skipping, kicking and hopping to the music. The rest of the crowd threw back their heads and sang their hearts out. I reckon even the people of New York, tucked up in their beds four thousand miles away, must have heard 'The Little Beggarman' that night.

A dark-eyed man in a smart suit joined the musicians on top of the table. He held a pear-shaped instrument I hadn't seen before and began plucking its strings with something that looked like a feather.

> *I slept in the barn down at Caurabawn,*
> *The night was wet and I slept till dawn,*
> *With holes in the roof and the rain*
> > *coming through*
> *And the rats and the cats, they were playing*
> > *peek-a-boo!*

Just as we sang the rats-and-cats bit, a real live rat streaked under the table and dashed among the dancers. People screamed and pointed. Some jumped onto chairs and tables and others rushed after the rat, laughing their heads off.

"Somebody catch it!" they cried.

I ducked and dodged through the crowd, closing in on the rat. I've caught a few rodents in my time and the secret is simple – don't try to chase it, head it off. And don't grab where it is, grab where it's *going* to be.

I dived to the floor and cupped my hands in front of the scurrying rat.

"*Gotcha!*" I cried, but I had spoken too soon. Another hand shot out in front of mine to grab the rat. Our heads banged together hard and I blacked out.

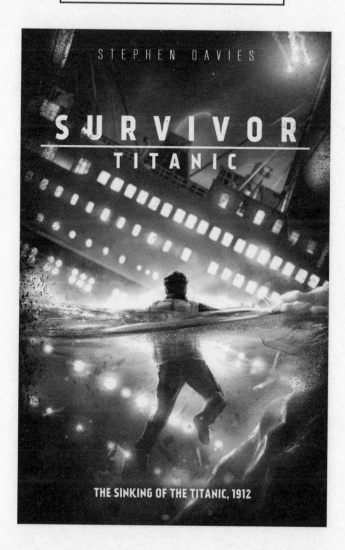

STEPHEN DAVIES

SURVIVOR
TITANIC

THE SINKING OF THE TITANIC, 1912